THE GOOSE EGG

Liz Wong

WITHDRAWN

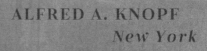

ALFRED A. KNOPF

New York

For Mom and for Nicholas

THIS IS A BORZOI BOOK PUBLISHED BY ALFRED A. KNOPF

Copyright © 2019 by Liz Wong

Visit us on the Web! rhcbooks.com

Educators and librarians, for a variety of teaching tools, visit us at
RHTeachersLibrarians.com

Library of Congress Cataloging-in-Publication Data is available upon request.

ISBN 978-0-553-51157-4 (trade) — ISBN 978-0-553-51158-1 (lib. bdg.) — ISBN 978-0-553-51159-8 (ebook)

The text of this book is set in 20-point Cabrito Didone.
The illustrations were created using watercolor, colored pencil, gouache, and a touch of Photoshop.

MANUFACTURED IN CHINA
January 2019
10 9 8 7 6 5 4 3 2 1

First Edition

Henrietta loved quiet.
  She savored the stillness of the
morning as she sipped her Darjeeling.
  She loved the soft rustle of the
newspaper as she turned its pages.

And more than anything, she
loved the lake. The lake could
be noisy on the surface.

But once Henrietta slipped below the surface, there was only the faint murmur of the water.

She lost herself in her thoughts.

Sometimes she got
a little *too* lost.

BONK!

Henrietta's thoughts scattered.
She went home to collect herself.

She gently felt her sore head.

What a lump! A real goose egg!

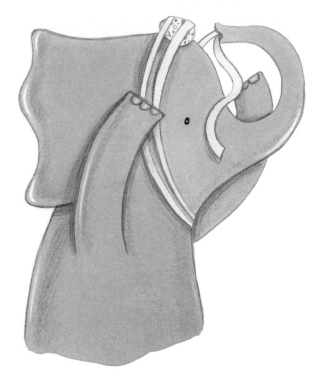

So she bandaged her head
and kept quiet, waiting for the
bump to heal.

Until . . .

CRACK!

She felt the top of her head.
She felt something soft.
Something fuzzy.
Something like . . .

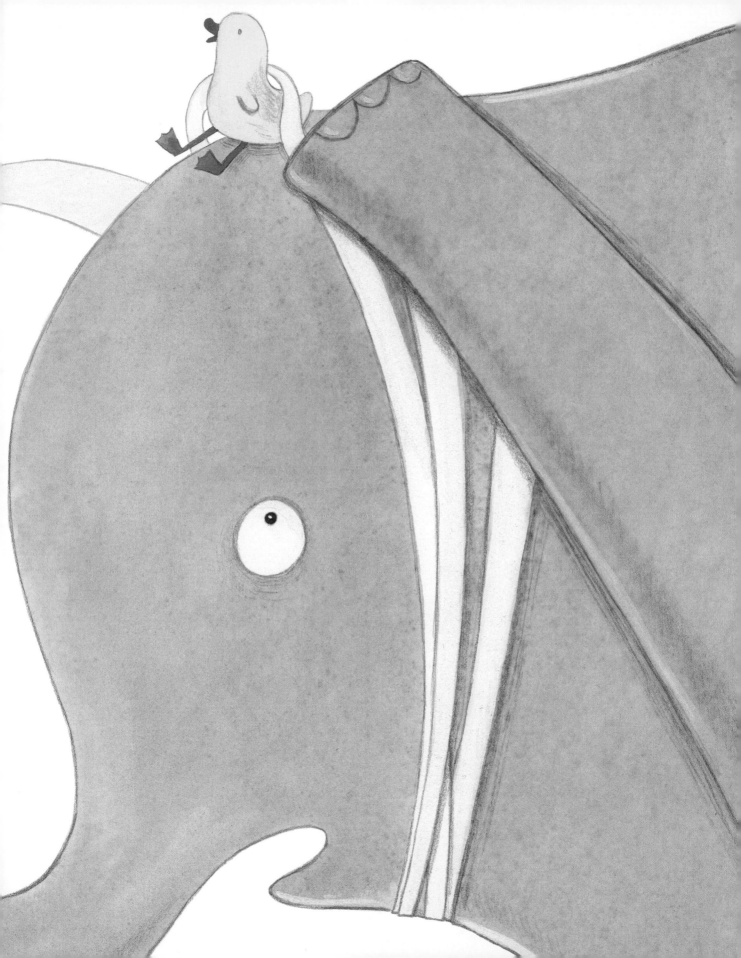

Henrietta ran back to the lake,
found a nest, and carefully
placed the baby goose inside.

Henrietta waited. And waited.

But no mother bird appeared.

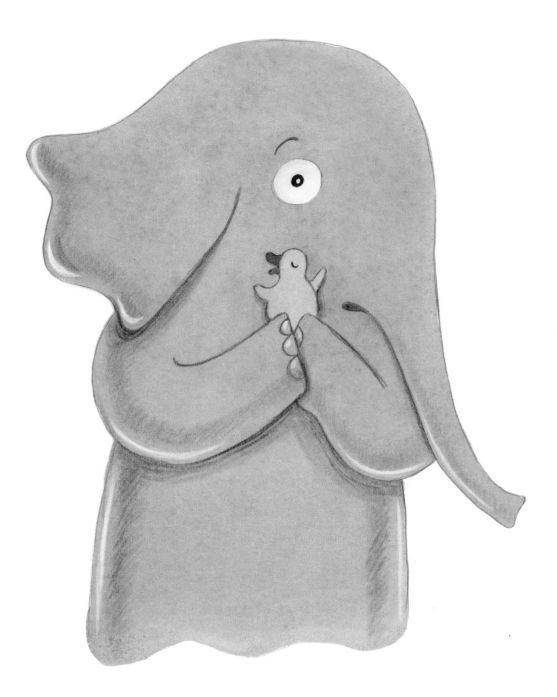

Henrietta couldn't just leave
poor Goose alone. She scooped
her up and took her home.

From then on, Henrietta's quiet was shattered.
Mornings were splashy instead of still. The
newspaper didn't rustle. It ripped.

Something needed to change.

And as Goose
got bigger, she
only got noisier.

Honk!

Honk!

And as Goose

Honk!
Honk!
Honk!

Henrietta realized
she had to teach
Goose to behave like
a proper goose.

So Henrietta hatched a plan.

She showed Goose how to look for food.

How to follow along.

How to flap her wings.

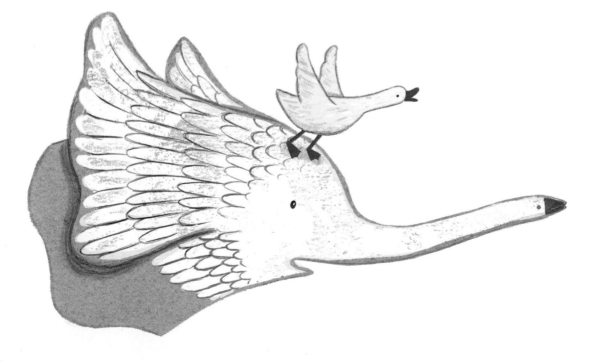

How to hang on.

And how to let go.

When Goose was grown,
it really was time
for her to go.

Bye, Goose!
You'll do great
out there!

Henrietta's house was quiet again.

But she found that
she didn't love the quiet
quite so much anymore.

And at night she dreamed
she heard Goose honking.

Then one day, the honking was real.

Henrietta loved those noisy goslings!

And the quiet was even better than before.